THIS IGLOO BOOK BELONGS TO:

....

igloobooks

Published in 2019
by Igloo Books Ltd, Cottage Farm, Sywell, NN6 0BJ
www.igloobooks.com

Copyright © 2018 Igloo Books Ltd
Igloo Books is an imprint of Bonnier Books UK

0819 001.01
2 4 6 8 10 9 7 5 3 1
ISBN 978-1-83852-151-6

Written by Melanie Joyce
Illustrated by César Samaniego

Designed by Alice Dainty
Edited by Kathryn Beer

Printed and manufactured in China

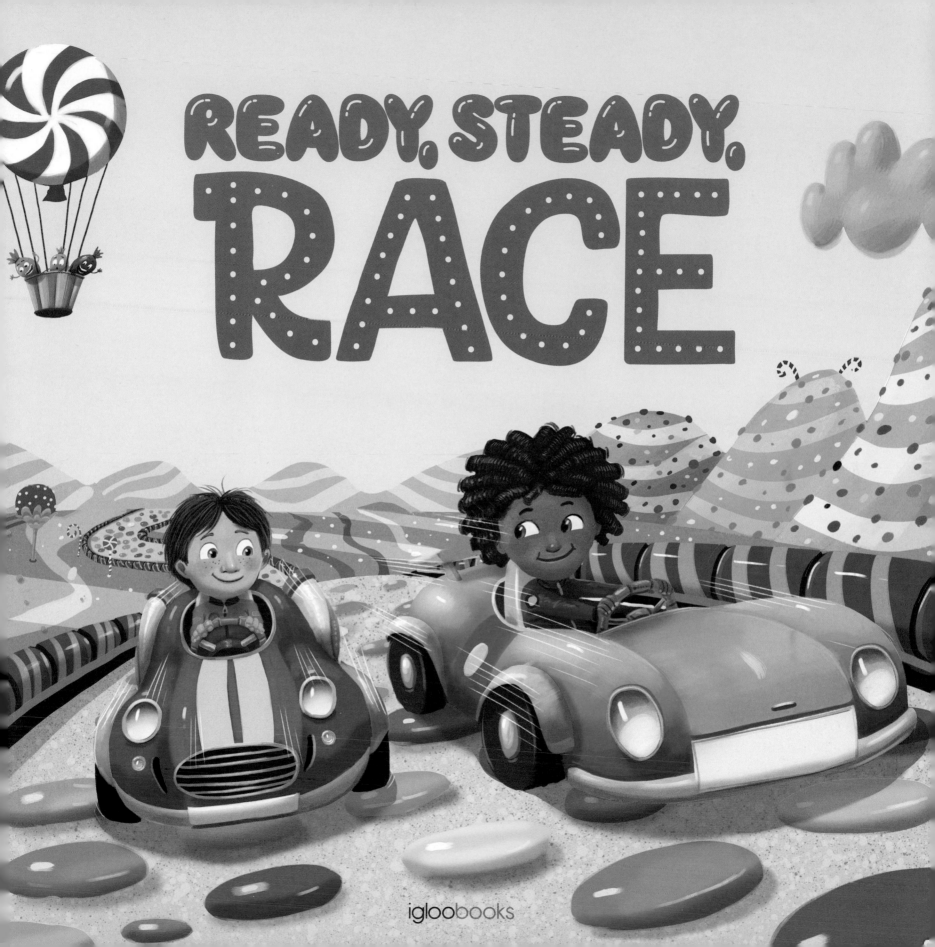

READY, STEADY, RACE

igloobooks

Here is Ed.

Here is Jo.

They're getting ready. It's time to go!

In race cars made with paint and glue...

... they fasten seat belts. One click, two.

Engines roar...

...vr**OO**m

vr**OO**m

vr**OO**m!

Ready, steady... off they

ZOOM!

Ed and Jo, side by side, on a...

...MAGICAL
race car ride!

Look at them go, Ed and Jo,
whizzing over the big rainbow.

Racing off down sugar lanes,
lined with **swirly** candy canes.

Past the caramel cookie trees.
"Hey," calls Jo,
"get some for me!"
Off they go, **speeding** away,
on their magical racing day.

Z-z-z-z

A chocolate train comes **clickety clack**,
chugging down the railway track.

Ed and Jo say,
"We'll race you!"

The chocolate train goes **WOO-WOO-WOO!**

Through marshmallow clouds they **fly**, tooting as they **WHIZZ** on by.

Past houses
made of gingerbread,
on they go,
full speed ahead.

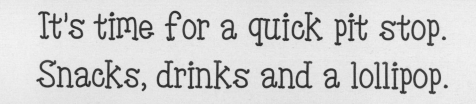

It's time for a quick pit stop.
Snacks, drinks and a lollipop.

They're off again, **speeding** away...

... but who will win the race today?

Jo's in front...

... and now it's Ed.

Then Jo again...

... then Ed's ahead!

Soon they reach the bright rainbow.
Vroom, vroom, vroom...

... over they go.

"I'll win!" cries Ed. **"The race is mine!"**
Jo **chases** him to the finish line.

They **rev** their engines and **vroom** some more...

... then cross the line. **It's a draw!**

Ed and Jo
are as happy as can be.
They've made it home
in time for tea!

They hug each other, smile and say,
"We loved our magical racing day!"

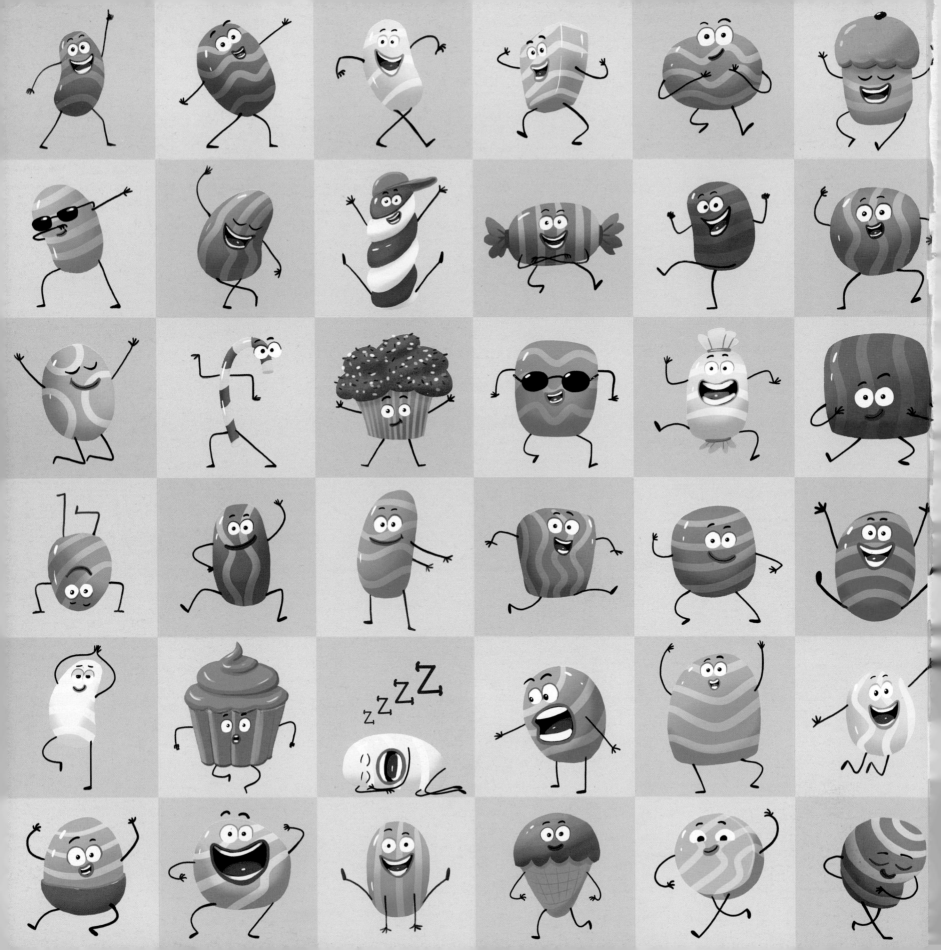